The Divided Light

Hakim Ibn Adam

ISBN: 978-1-9990656-3-8

DEDICATION

For the patient minds who doubt with reverence,
And bold hearts who dare to think what cannot be said—
May your path lead not to certainty,
But to the quiet knowing that waits beyond it.

CONTENTS

ACKNOWLEDGMENTS

This book could not have come into being without the silent companionship of many souls—living and departed—whose thoughts, questions, and dreams whispered through the margins of my reading and the silences of my reflection. I am deeply indebted to the many scientists, philosophers, and mystics cited in the appendix, whose foundational work provided the intellectual and contemplative landscape for this journey.

1

THE CELL THAT HESITATED

Hakim Ibn Adam watched thousands of cells die through his microscope that morning, but one T-lymphocyte refused to behave like chemistry.

His laboratory hummed with the white noise of incubators and laminar flow hoods. The confocal microscope's lasers painted his immune cells in false colors—nuclei glowing blue with DAPI stain, cytoplasm green with calcein-AM, mitochondria pulsing red with MitoTracker. He'd been running the same apoptosis assay for months, treating activated T-cells with staurosporine to trigger programmed cell death, watching them shrink and fragment with clockwork precision.

The protocol was routine: harvest peripheral blood

mononuclear cells, activate with anti-CD3 and anti-CD28 antibodies, culture for 72 hours until they bloomed into eager killers, then add 1 μM staurosporine and document their orderly suicide. Within six hours, phosphatidylserine would flip to the outer membrane—the cellular equivalent of a white flag. Caspase-3 would activate, chopping cellular proteins with enzymatic precision. The nucleus would condense, fragment, and the cell would package itself into tidy apoptotic bodies for neighboring phagocytes to consume.

But cell #302 stalled.

For the past three hours, he'd watched it refuse its programmed death. Where others had begun the characteristic blebbing of early apoptosis, their membranes bubbling like water beginning to boil, this cell remained smooth. Its mitochondria, which should have been fragmenting as cytochrome c leaked out to trigger the death cascade, continued their steady fusion-fission cycles. The JC-1 dye showed their membrane potential holding steady, with red aggregates still dominating over green monomers.

More intriguing still were its stress granules. He'd added arsenite to induce oxidative stress alongside the staurosporine, expecting to see the classic aggregation of G3BP1 and TIA-1 proteins into discrete cytoplasmic foci. In neighboring cells, these granules formed and dissolved with predictable kinetics—liquid-liquid phase separation in action, proteins condensing like morning dew when RNA metabolism stalled.

But this cell's stress granules flickered. They'd begin to nucleate—he could see the G3BP1-GFP puncta starting to form—then dissolve before reaching the critical size threshold. Reform. Dissolve. As if the cell were testing different configurations, weighing options.

He increased magnification, watching the intrinsically disordered regions of G3BP1 sample conformations. These proteins had no fixed structure—their disorder was their function, allowing them to serve as molecular velcro, binding RNA and other proteins in combinatorial complexity. The phase transition should have been straightforward physics: when the local concentration exceeded the saturation point, condensation occurred. Like salt crystallizing from a supersaturated solution.

Cell *#302* seemed to be actively tuning its phase diagram. Post-translational modifications flickered across the proteins—phosphorylation events visible as subtle changes in GFP fluorescence. The cell was rewriting its own responsiveness in real-time, adjusting the critical concentration needed for granule formation.

He switched to calcium imaging, loading the cells with Fluo-4. Calcium transients sparked through the rebellious cell, but not the sustained elevation that typically preceded apoptosis. Instead, he saw oscillations. Waves of calcium release from endoplasmic reticulum stores, each spike activating different transcription factors. NFAT, NF-κB, CREB—each responding to specific calcium signatures like musicians following a conductor's tempo.

The cell was not simply failing to die. It was computing.

He zoomed in further, following the dance of individual protein complexes. The mTOR pathway, which should have been shutting down under stress, showed sporadic activity. Bursts of mTORC1 assembly on lysosomal surfaces, recruiting substrates, phosphorylating S6K and 4E-BP1, then dispersing. The cell was sampling different metabolic states, testing whether growth was still possible despite the death signals.

At the nucleus, he watched transcription factors trafficking in and out with unusual patterns. P53, the guardian of the genome, accumulated as expected in response to DNA damage. But instead of driving the classic apoptotic program, it seemed caught in a feedback loop with MDM2. Pulses of p53 activity, each pulse querying the cell's state, each answer modulating the next pulse's amplitude.

The gene regulatory network was integrating signals from dozens of pathways—DNA damage checkpoints, metabolic sensors, stress responses, and survival cascades. The genome wasn't issuing commands but engaged in a complex negotiation with the cytoplasm. Chromatin remodeling complexes slid along DNA, opening and closing regulatory regions. Pioneer transcription factors sampled closed chromatin, occasionally prying open new sites of possibility.

He had published papers dissecting these mechanisms with the cold precision of a watchmaker examining gears. Signal transduction was biochemistry, nothing more. Kinases phosphorylate substrates with rate constants determined by thermodynamics. Transcription factors bind DNA with affinities measured in nanomolar dissociation constants. Even the liquid-liquid phase separation of stress granules follows the mean-field theory of polymer solutions.

But watching this singular cell navigate the molecular decision tree of death, something shifted in his perception. The question arrived like an intruder in his ordered world:

What dreams through these molecules?

He rubbed his eyes—hours of staring at screens left them dry and strained. The familiar smell of DMEM medium and the sharp ozone scent from the lasers suddenly seemed overwhelming. He was adjusting the focus, trying to capture the cell's nuclear morphology in greater detail, when the first *wave of vertigo* hit.

The fluorescent image on the monitor began to pulse—not the steady data acquisition he'd programmed but something organic, rhythmic. The cell's calcium oscillations, usually a reassuring 0.1 Hz wave on his analysis software, seemed to slow and deepen. Each spike now lasted subjective minutes, though the timestamp showed seconds still ticking normally.

His hands on the focus knobs felt strange—too large, too clumsy, as if he were wearing thick gloves. The latex gloves he actually wore seemed to dissolve, leaving his skin hypersensitive to every ridge on the metal controls. The laboratory's temperature, regulated to exactly 20°C, fluctuated wildly against his skin—arctic cold, then fever-warm, then something beyond temperature altogether.

The edges of his vision began to shimmer. The computer monitors, the shelves of reagents, the familiar geometry of the lab—all of it developed halos of impossible color. Not quite ultraviolet, not quite infrared, but something his visual cortex had no name for. The fluorescent proteins in his cells were bleeding their colors into the room. Cyan foxes darted across his peripheral vision. Scarlet serpents of mitochondria writhed on the walls.

Sound became visible. The hum of the incubators painted amber spirals in the air. The whisper of laminar flow drew silver threads across space. His own heartbeat emerged as expanding spheres of deep burgundy, each pulse revealing the room in a different configuration—now vast as a cathedral, now small as the inside of a cell.

He tried to stand, to step back from the microscope, but his legs wouldn't respond properly. No—that wasn't right. They responded too well, reported too much. He could feel every muscle fiber, every motor unit firing in sequence. The propagation of action potentials down his sciatic nerve was a river of lightning he could track in real-time. His proprioceptors screamed data about joint angles and muscle tension that his brain had never consciously processed before.

The cell on the screen pulsed larger, or he shrank smaller—the distinction lost meaning. The boundary between his eye and the eyepiece dissolved first, then the distinction between retina and camera, between his visual cortex and the image processing software. He wasn't looking at the cell anymore. The looking had collapsed into something more immediate.

He was inside cell #302.

The cytoplasm pressed against him—not wet but somehow liquid, a three-dimensional maze of proteins and membranes. He could taste the pH, slightly alkaline, fluctuating as metabolic reactions churned around him. The viscosity was everything and nothing like water—Brownian motion buffeted him with the force of hurricanes, yet movement felt more like swimming through honey that thought.

A mitochondrion loomed before him, vast as a subway tunnel, its cristae folding in on themselves in fractal complexity. He could hear it—the electron transport chain singing as electrons tumbled down energy gradients, ATP synthase spinning with a high keening note, protons flooding through like a Bach fugue played on the universe's smallest organ. The sound had color—deep purple shot through with electric blue—and the color had texture, crystalline and soft simultaneously.

Stress granules bloomed around him like storm clouds, proteins condensing from the cytoplasmic solution. But from inside, he understood—they weren't passive condensation. Each protein carried memory, probability, and potential. G3BP1 molecules reached for each other with arms made of disorder, testing configurations, and computing outcomes.

It was decision, not physics—choice, not chance.

And yet—even as the words formed in his mind, he felt their double edge. Perhaps what he witnessed was only stochastic patterning, interpreted through the lens of a mind desperate for meaning. Perhaps this was metaphor—projected agency layered onto molecular dynamics. But if so, it was a metaphor born not from ignorance but from resonance, from some deep symmetry between his own interiority and the processes unfolding before him. Maybe the cell wasn't thinking, but something was, through it.

The nucleus rose before him, its envelope riddled with nuclear pores like mouths, speaking proteins in and out with purpose he could almost grasp. Through one pore, he slipped—or was pulled, or chose to enter. The distinction between his agency and the cell's dissolved like cream in coffee.

Inside the nucleus, DNA wasn't a ladder or a string but a vast library written in light. Each base pair glowed with meaning that transcended chemistry—adenine singing to thymine in harmonies that were love songs, guanine and cytosine locked in conversations that spanned billions of years. Histones embraced the double helix like protective parents, loosening and tightening their grip as the cell decided which stories to read, which futures to write.

He witnessed p53 arriving like a detective at a crime scene, assessing damage with molecular fingers, conferring with repair enzymes in a language of conformational changes. The decision—repair or die—hung in the nuclear space like a question mark made of phosphorylation cascades. And he understood, with the clarity of direct experience, that this wasn't mechanical. The cell was *choosing*, weighing options with a calculus that included but transcended chemistry.

Time folded. He experienced the cell's history—its birth from a hematopoietic stem cell, its education in the thymus where it learned self from non-self, its activation by antigen, its proliferation into an army of clones. But also its future— all potential fates spreading before it like a garden of forking paths. Death was one path, survival another, but there were stranger options too. Transformation. Transcendence. Becoming something unprecedented.

A calcium wave approached—from inside, it wasn't a signal but a shout of silver fire. It washed through him/the cell, and suddenly he could feel what calcium felt—the urgency of a universe trying to communicate through the narrow bandwidth of electron shells. Every ion carried information from the beginning of time, remembered the stars that forged it, the supernovae that scattered it, the aeons of geology that concentrated it, and the evolution that learned to use it as language.

The wave crested, and—*He was back*. Slumped in his chair, both hands gripping the optical table so hard his knuckles had gone white. The clock showed three minutes had passed. Three minutes. The timestamp on his data acquisition confirmed it—180 seconds of normal recording. But his muscles ached like he'd been clenched for hours. His throat was raw as if he'd been screaming or singing or both.

On the monitor, cell #302 continued its dance between death and decision. But now he could see what the instruments couldn't measure—the interiority of it, the felt experience of molecular choice. His hands shook as he reached for his notebook, trying to capture something that had no words in any human language.

The question that had been lurking at the edges of his research for months now stood naked before him, terrible in its simplicity: If *consciousness* could recognize itself in the dance of cellular proteins, then what exactly had he been studying all these years—*mechanism or mind*?

But even that question seemed too small now. The real question, the one that made his teeth ache and his vision blur, was simpler and more devastating:

What if there had never been a difference?

The question hung in the sterile air like incense in a cathedral—foreign and sacred and utterly heretical. Cells did not possess consciousness. This was the first commandment of modern biology, the bedrock upon which his entire career had been built. Consciousness belonged to complex nervous systems, billions of neurons firing in patterns too intricate for mathematics to map.

He caught his reflection in the dark computer monitor— pupils still dilated, his pulse hammered at 120 bpm according to his smartwatch, though it was already beginning to slow. He looked exactly like himself and entirely like a stranger.

On the main screen, the other cells in the field continued their programmed deaths with mechanical precision. Membrane blebbing, nuclear fragmentation, the orderly packaging of cellular contents—all proceeding exactly as his thousands of previous experiments had documented. Only cell #302 persisted in its refusal, a single point of rebellion in a field of conformity.

His hands trembled as he saved the image sequence—hours of cellular decision-making captured in time-lapse. The gesture felt final, though he couldn't say why. Perhaps some part of him already knew this was the last night he would see cells as *mere mechanisms.*

He pulled away from the microscope and stood in the empty laboratory, surrounded by the expensive tools of reductionist certainty. But what if they had been asking the wrong questions all along?

The anomalous cell had done more than defy his models. It had revealed the models themselves as elaborate fictions, mathematical poetry that described the shadow play on the cave wall while the real performance happened elsewhere, in dimensions no equation could capture.

Consciousness.

The word lingered—unspoken, unsettling—a heresy against everything science demanded. Yet what else could explain the behavior he'd documented? What else could account for what he'd just experienced?

If consciousness meant sensing, processing information, making decisions, learning from experience—if it meant the capacity to respond creatively to novel situations, to integrate past and present into adaptive futures—then what was this cellular behavior he'd been documenting?

The thought was perhaps fatal to a career built on mechanistic certainties. But here, alone with the humming machines and the decision-making cell, he could acknowledge what his heart had been murmuring for months:

Reality was far stranger than measurement could contain.

Maybe the clean distinctions between observer and observed, subject and object, mind and matter, were conveniences, not truths—Elegant fictions that science had mistaken for reality itself.

2

THE LIBRARY AT MIDNIGHT

Hakim's study at home was his sanctuary, though tonight it felt more like a mausoleum. The leather of his chair had molded to his form over decades, forming a negative space that held his questioning.

Books rose from floor to ceiling in stratified layers—the geological record of humanity's attempt to capture truth in words. The bottom shelves groaned under the weight of science texts with their confident diagrams, evolutionary treatises mapping life's branching rivers, and cosmology volumes that reduced the universe to equations elegant as symphonies and cold as starlight.

The middle shelves held philosophy's restless spirits—Descartes dreaming his methodical doubt, Hume sharpening skepticism to a blade that cut through everything, including itself, Kant building his elaborate prison of categories and concepts, and several others. And above, in the dusty heights, waited the books of mystics and theologians, their spines faded and pages yellowed.

He sank into his leather chair as midnight approached, the single desk lamp casting a golden circle in an ocean of shadows. The lamplight pooled on the page like amber preserving ancient intentions. He would begin at the beginning, with the world that had once made perfect sense.

The Newtonian cosmos beckoned first, not as choice but as gravity, his mind falling toward the familiar comfort of equations. Here was reality as a crystalline lattice, each atom a note in a score written by no composer, performed for no audience. *Space*: the eternal auditorium. *Time*: the metronome that never tires. And dancing to this soundless music, particles traced their deterministic ballet, their future positions calculable from their past, their behavior governed by laws as immutable as scripture but far more reliable.

The vision had intoxicated humanity for three centuries. Here, at last, was a world that could be grasped, predicted, controlled. No capricious deities, no mysterious purposes, no final causes drawing things toward their destiny. Just matter in motion, following rules that any mind could comprehend and any mathematics could express.

But even as he clung to this clarity, a whisper arose—not from the books but from the space between heartbeats:

Who hears this cosmic silence? Who watches the unwatched dance?

The question drew him inexorably to Descartes. That surgical mind had tried to solve this puzzle by splitting reality down the middle with precision that left no rough edges. On one side: *res extensa*, the extended substance, matter that occupied space and obeyed mechanical laws. On the other: *res cogitans*, the thinking substance, the mind that existed without location and operated by the laws of reason and will. The solution was elegant as a mathematical proof—it preserved both the mechanical universe that science required and the conscious self that experience revealed.

But the wound this division opened had never healed. By making mind and matter two completely different substances, Descartes had made their obvious interaction incomprehensible. He had saved consciousness only by exiling it from the physical world, leaving it to float like a ghost above the machine it could somehow direct but never truly touch.

What if the division itself was the error?

The lamplight flickered—or perhaps it was his vision, overwrought with seeking. His eyes fell on a volume of cell biology history, and he remembered how this same schism had infected biology from its birth as a modern science.

When Hooke first glimpsed those cork cells, what did he truly see? Empty rooms, he thought—*cellula*—architectural absence waiting to be filled. But perhaps he had stumbled upon the universe's most profound koan: form revealing emptiness, emptiness manifesting as form. Each cell is a meditation chamber where matter learned to think itself into being.

Leeuwenhoek's "animalcules" danced in their drop of pond water like thoughts—too small for theology to notice, too alive for mechanism to explain. Were they discovering life, or was life discovering itself through their astonished eyes?

The progression from Hooke's static cork cells to Schleiden and Schwann's universal cell theory to Virchow's insight that all cells arise from pre-existing cells—each discovery had seemed to solidify the mechanistic view. Life was cellular machinery following physical laws. But now, three and a half centuries after Hooke first peered through his crude microscope, the machinery itself was revealing something that transcended mechanism.

What if the machine metaphor itself was the problem?

By the twentieth century, the genome became the new *res cogitans*—pure information directing passive matter. DNA issued commands to cellular machinery just as Descartes' mind commanded the body. Information flowed in one direction only, from genes to proteins to organisms, with life reduced to "survival machines" built by and for their genetic programs. It was Cartesian dualism in molecular drag—

mind replaced by genetic program, but the same fundamental separation between controller and controlled, ghost and machine.

But the deeper Hakim looked into cellular behavior, the more this picture crumbled. Evidence came from biological rhythms, where the supposed hierarchy of genetic control revealed itself as elaborate fiction. Downward causation was everywhere once you learned to see it. The molecular and the systemic were co-determining, each level constraining and enabling the others in an endless recursive loop.

The stress granules, these membraneless organelles formed through phase transitions when cells experienced stress, but their formation was actively regulated by the cell itself. Critical concentrations weren't fixed physical constants but changed dynamically based on cellular conditions. The cell was actively regulating its own phase transitions, using granules as both sensors and effectors in sophisticated stress management.

The parts were creating the whole that organized the parts.

The implications arrived not as understanding but as vertigo. Hakim gripped the chair's arms as his conceptual world inverted: the whole determining its parts, which created the whole which... The sentence could not complete itself. This wasn't failure of language but language discovering its own strange loop, thought thinking itself into existence through the very proteins it claimed to explain.

Another hour dissolved in the amber light, leaving only the

residue of inadequate answers. If genes were switches, what was doing the switching? If proteins were signals, what was interpreting them? If cells were circuits, what was performing the computation?

Every mechanistic explanation required something that was not itself mechanical—some integrating principle that could read signals, interpret information, and coordinate responses. The ghost was back, but now it haunted every level of biological organization.

These examples pointed toward a deeper principle that overturned the mechanistic worldview:

Biological causation was irreducibly circular.

In living systems, there was no clear hierarchy from genes to proteins to cells to organisms. Instead, each level constrained and enabled every other through complex feedback relationships.

If causation were circular rather than linear, if higher-level properties constrained lower-level processes just as much as lower-level processes generated higher-level properties, then reductionism—the core methodology of modern science—would not only be incomplete but fundamentally misguided.

The whole was not just greater than the sum of its parts—it was a different kind of thing entirely.

What if life were not a special case of chemistry but

chemistry's awakening to creative intelligence?

What if the circular causality he perceived reflected not computational complexity but conscious agency expressing itself through biochemical processes? What if "emergence" was actually the manifestation of a deeper organizing principle that became increasingly apparent as systems grew more complex?

The ghost was not in the machine—the ghost was the machine dreaming itself into ever-greater complexity.

The recognition was both intellectually rigorous and utterly mystical. The most cutting-edge science was validating the most ancient wisdom: the cosmos was not dead matter occasionally infected by mind, but mind itself, exploring its own infinite creative potential through every level of organization.

But knowing about it was not the same as knowing it directly.

All these examples of downward causation and circular causality were still maps—more accurate than the old mechanistic ones, but maps nonetheless. The truth they pointed toward couldn't be found in any description of regulatory networks or phase transitions. It had to be lived, experienced, and recognized through direct participation of consciousness in its own creative processes.

The books stood around him like a tribunal of beautiful failures—each one a magnificent attempt to cage the uncageable.

He was not studying the ghost in the machine. He was the ghost, dreaming machinery into existence. He was the machine, waking to find itself haunted. He was the dreaming and the waking and the space between, where all paradoxes dissolved into simple presence.

The clock prepared to chime again, but time had become strange—not Newton's uniform flow but something that pooled and eddied around moments of recognition. He could sit here forever, suspended between one heartbeat and the next, or he could rise and carry this terrible knowledge back into the world of daylight certainties.

Neither choice was his to make. The choosing was already happening, had always been happening, in dimensions no map could chart.

3

MAPS OF THE UNMAPPABLE

The silver note of the clock dissolved into silence. One in the morning—the hour when the mind's careful architectures begin their slow collapse, when the guards of reason sleep and stranger truths slip through.

Hakim's fingers found Hume before his mind chose him—the leather binding soft as doubt itself, worn smooth by decades of questioning. The book opened to familiar devastations, each page a small apocalypse of certainty. His pulse synchronized with doubt—each heartbeat a question mark, each breath an erasure.

If all knowledge comes from experience, what can we truly know?

The question no longer lived in abstract space but in his viscera. His cellular observations had shattered the comfortable certainties of mechanistic biology, but what if Hume was right? What if the "intelligence" he perceived in cells was just another habit of mind, another projection onto the flux of molecular events?

Hume's logic entered him like a virus, dismantling cellular certainties one protein at a time. Watch one billiard ball strike another—but where was the invisible thread of causation? Only sequence, only habit, only the mind's desperate weaving of connection where none could be proven.

His own hand on the page became suspect. What moved it? Not will—will was just another sensation among sensations. Not self—the self dissolved under examination.

Just as I never see the cellular "decision" itself, only the before and after.

The parallel struck with physical force. The stress granules he'd observed—had they truly "responded" to cellular stress? Or had he merely witnessed coincidence dressed in the costume of causation? The thought made his teeth ache.

When he observed stress granules forming, what was he actually witnessing? Protein concentrations rising above critical thresholds, phase transitions occurring according to thermodynamic principles, and molecular assemblies appearing with statistical regularity. But the moment of cellular "assessment"—that integration of multiple signals, that weighted calculation—remained as invisible as Hume's missing causation.

Perhaps he had been mistaking correlation for agency. The cell didn't "choose" to form granules any more than the second billiard ball "chose" to move when struck by the first. Every equation he'd ever written assumed the reliability of cause and effect. But perhaps cellular intelligence was just another projection, another habit of mind imposed upon molecular flux.

The thought was devastating—If causation was merely mental habit, then his conviction about cellular consciousness might be nothing more than anthropomorphic bias, pattern-seeking gone pathological.

But Hume's demolition didn't stop with the external world. Turning inward, what remained? No stable self—only a flux of perceptions succeeding each other with bewildering rapidity. The self was not the observer of this stream but merely another name for the stream itself.

I think, therefore I am? But what is this "I" that thinks?

If there was no permanent self, what was conducting his science? Perhaps consciousness itself was just another event in the stream of causeless happenings, a bubble in foam believing itself the eternal ocean.

It was rigorous. It was honest. And it was intolerable.

The room spun as if gravity had changed direction. Someone had to rebuild what Hume dismantled. Someone had to save science from skepticism, knowledge from dissolution, the observing mind from annihilation. That someone had been Immanuel Kant, the sage of Königsberg whose thoughts journeyed to the limits of human reason without leaving his hometown.

Hume's skepticism had awakened Kant from his "dogmatic slumber," forcing him to ask: How is knowledge possible at all?

The Kantian revolution struck like a sudden pressure change, ears popping as conceptual altitude shifted. He wasn't finding order in the universe; he was secreting it like a spider secretes a web, then marveling at the patterns.
The recognition hit with nauseating clarity. We don't discover *space* and *time* in the world; we impose them upon it. They are lenses through which perception occurs, no more removable than the eyes that see.

His cellular observations rearranged themselves backward:

Not "I see the cell deciding" but "I project decision onto molecular flux."

And beyond the forms of intuition lay Kant's categories of understanding—causality, substance, agency—not windows but stained glass, coloring everything with the hues of human cognition.

Mind didn't passively receive a world of causes and effects; it actively constructed such a world. *We are not spectators of the show but co-creators of it.*

When he observed "cellular decisions," was he discovering something in the cells themselves, or imposing the category of agency upon molecular events? The categories of his understanding—causality, substance, necessity—these weren't empirical discoveries but transcendental conditions, the conceptual framework that mind applied to sensation to construct coherent experience.

Kant had saved science by grounding its universal laws not in external reality but in mind itself. Of course, we find causation everywhere—we put it there through categorical understanding. Of course, the world appears orderly—order is our contribution, not a discovery about mind-independent reality.

But the price of this salvation was exile from reality itself.

The ache traveled from Hakim's teeth to temple to chest, skepticism manifesting as pain. Kant's prison revealed itself not as a building but as body—the bars were his own ribs, the walls his own skull. He could map every dimension of his cell because the cell was him. The *Ding an sich* (the "thing-in-itself") lurked beyond like a sound too low to hear but felt in the bones, a presence known only by the shape of its absence.

If we know only the world filtered through our forms of intuition and categories of understanding, what of the world as it actually is?

The notorious *thing-in-itself* remained forever unknowable, absolutely inaccessible, necessarily beyond all possible experience.

And what did this mean for consciousness studying itself?

How could the very faculty that imposed categories upon experience turn those same categories upon itself? If consciousness were the condition of all knowledge, it could never become an object of knowledge without ceasing to be consciousness.

Heat rose from the floorboards like fever as the post-Kantian philosophers attempted their escapes. Hegel declared the prison a palace, making consciousness and reality identical through Spirit's historical self-recognition. But whose Spirit? And why should cosmic consciousness follow a German professor's logic?

The air grew thick as syrup, each breath a struggle against meaning's viscosity. The postmodernists arrived, not destroying the structure but revealing it had always been hollow. Words eating words, meaning devouring its own tail. When he thought "cell," what was he thinking? Not the thing itself but a node in a network of differences—not-virus, not-molecule, not-organism. The cellular "self" existed only as a linguistic phantom, a ghost made of grammar.

His own sense of agency began to fray. Was "Hakim Ibn

Adam" anything more than a discursive construction, a story consciousness told itself while automated processes masqueraded as choice? The thought should have been terrifying, but terror required a self to feel it, and the self had become another text awaiting deconstruction.

The stress granules were never encountered directly but always through mediating apparatus—protocols, instruments, and theoretical frameworks. The "intelligence" emerged only through differential comparisons: stressed versus unstressed, before versus after. Perhaps the "living cell" was never simply present but was constituted through its differences—from dead matter, from other cells, from previous states.

Foucault whispered that knowledge was power, that the techniques making cellular behavior visible were simultaneously techniques of control. The "intelligent cell" might not be a discovery but a discursive production, called into being by the very apparatus studying it.

The postmodern critique was comprehensive, relentless, and ultimately self-consuming.

If every truth claim was suspect, every concept a construction, every observation mediated, every interpreter an effect rather than origin, what remained? Only endless vigilance against believing anything with conviction.

Philosophy had eaten itself, devouring every premise, beckoning us to question what remains when all certainties dissolve.

The journey had led from confident mechanism through skeptical dissolution to transcendental imprisonment, from systematic construction to nihilistic deconstruction.

And where had it left him? Floating in a void of his own making, watching the instruments of his liberation become the bars of an even more subtle cage. Every path led to the same dead end: the impossibility of knowledge knowing itself, consciousness trying to catch its own tail in an endless recursion of mirrors.

The lamplight flickered—or perhaps it was his sanity. The awareness that had been analyzing all these philosophical positions remained, but now it seemed more like a curse than a gift. To be awake in a world where all awakening was suspect, to seek truth with tools that dissolved truth itself.

He sat in the wreckage of Western thought, surrounded by the scattered fragments of every certainty he'd ever held. The cellular intelligence he'd thought he'd discovered lay in ruins alongside causation, selfhood, and the possibility of genuine knowledge.

If this was where philosophy led—to the complete dissolution of everything, including the philosopher—then what hope was there?

4

CROSSING THE DIVIDE

Two in the morning. The void had revealed its teeth, and philosophy lay in ruins around him. Yet something in that devastation called to him—not the comfortable destruction of skepticism, but the creative possibilities hidden in collapse itself.

His hands trembled as they reached for the next volume. Not from exhaustion but from approaching something that demanded more than thinking. Decades of careful construction had crumbled, but perhaps that clearing was necessary. Perhaps some truths could only be born in the space where philosophy died.

What did it mean to be a scientist if knowledge itself was suspect?

What did it mean to study cells if consciousness couldn't study consciousness?

The leather binding of Kierkegaard fell open to a passage that had waited decades for this moment:

"Truth is subjectivity."

The words entered him like a fever. The Danish philosopher's intensity no longer lived on the page but in his bloodstream, each pulse carrying the message deeper: the most important questions could never be answered through objective analysis.

Truth wasn't discovered through universal reasoning but lived through passionate, individual commitment. In his own case, this meant that no amount of data about stress granules or gene regulatory networks could force the conclusion that cells were conscious agents.

The recognition struck like lightning, finding ground. His moment at the microscope—when cellular boundaries had dissolved and observer and observed merged in pure experiencing—that couldn't be argued for or proven. It could only be lived through the subjective intensity of direct encounter.

Kierkegaard's stages weren't abstractions but territories he could feel beneath his feet:

The *aesthetic*—here he stood now, collecting beautiful data like butterflies pinned to boards, publishing papers that were exercises in elegant emptiness. His hands knew this territory intimately: the smooth surface of success that never quite touched the depths. Each citation another ornament on a hollow tree, each award another weight preventing flight.

The *ethical* loomed like a gray cathedral—accepting the consensus, genuflecting before the altar of mechanistic materialism. He could taste it: ash and safety, the flavor of a soul choosing comfort over truth. To cross into this territory meant accepting the professional consensus, reducing cells to clockwork, consciousness to computation. Safe. Respectable. Soul-crushing.

But the *religious* stage... it yawned before him like the edge of a cliff in fog. The "teleological suspension of the ethical"—words too polite for what they demanded. Here was the territory beyond maps, where academic suicide became spiritual birth, where losing everything might be the only way to find what mattered.

Jump, whispered Kierkegaard through decades of dust.

Jump and trust the falling itself to teach you flight.

The leap terrified him because it wasn't metaphorical. It meant abandoning the coordinates of career, reputation, the comfortable identity he'd spent decades constructing.

Yet what was the alternative? To pretend he hadn't seen what he'd seen? To bury that moment of cellular communion under footnotes and grant proposals?

But even Kierkegaard's passionate subjectivity pointed beyond itself, toward something absolute that thought couldn't contain.

Nietzsche arrived through biological metaphor rather than cultural demolition. When Hakim observed neutrophils hunting bacteria, their pseudopodia reaching like liquid fingers, engulfing, destroying, incorporating—was this mere chemistry following thermodynamic gradients? Or was it *will* learning to *will* through membrane and cytoplasm?

Will to Power—not the crude domination of popular misunderstanding, but something subtler: the drive to grow, to overcome resistance, to discharge strength in creative self-expression. Life itself refusing the passive role that mechanism assigned to it.

When stem cells differentiated, choosing neural fate over muscle, blood over bone—was this biological programming or creative self-assertion at the molecular scale? The stress response he'd documented wasn't submission to environmental pressure but cellular defiance:

I will maintain homeostasis. I will adapt. I will survive and transform.

Not the crude competition of social Darwinism but something more sophisticated: creative force expressing itself through whatever forms enhanced its capacity to create.

Perhaps consciousness wasn't the exception but the rule—

matter's way of experiencing its own creative potential from the inside out. This insight opened a door he hadn't known existed.

But *will* carried the scent of struggle, the individual asserting against the world. What Hakim observed in cellular behavior suggested something more musical—creative force expressing itself through harmonies as much as solos, through collective improvisation as much as individual assertion.

What if consciousness wasn't an accident that occasionally infected dead matter? What if matter itself was consciousness exploring what it was like to be material, structural, alive?

The stress granules forming through phase separation, the gene regulatory networks processing information, the collective cellular migration—all might be consciousness learning how to be biological, each form a new experiment in awareness.

Henri Bergson had glimpsed this through his concept of *élan vital*—not a mystical addition to matter but matter's own tendency toward increasing complexity and consciousness.

Bergson's duration arrived like music—not the notation but the lived melody where past notes haunted present ones and future phrases called backward through time.

He felt it in his own cells: how yesterday's inflammation

informed today's immune response, how ancestral encounters with pathogens echoed in current antibody production. The present wasn't a knife-edge but a river carrying its entire history, pregnant with every possible future.

When proteins folded, they weren't following a predetermined script but improvising—ancient structural memories meeting present chemical conditions to create unprecedented configurations. This was creative evolution: not a ladder toward complexity but consciousness composing itself in real time, each moment a new verse in an endless song.

The phase transitions he studied—proteins condensing into droplets, dissolving back into solution—these weren't mechanical processes but durational ones. The past shaped the present probability landscape, and future needs called certain configurations into being. Time wasn't Newton's uniform flow but Bergson's lived duration, thick with memory and swollen with possibility.

Life was neither a mechanism nor a predetermined plan but a creative advance into novelty.

The philosophical journey was revealing something profound: every attempt to solve the mystery of consciousness through thinking led to the same recognition. Whether Kierkegaard's leap beyond reason, Nietzsche's creative will's self-assertion, or Bergson's creative evolution—all pointed toward something that couldn't be captured in concepts.

The mystery wasn't a problem to be solved, but the mysterious source of all problem-solving.

His moment at the microscope hadn't been a temporary lapse of scientific objectivity. It had been a glimpse of the reality that thinking could point toward but never contain.

The books around him—all of them, centuries of human reaching—suddenly revealed their secret: they weren't maps to somewhere else but fingers pointing beyond themselves.

Like Kierkegaard's leap, like Nietzsche's creative force, like Bergson's duration—all were gestures toward a territory that philosophy could only approach but never enter.

The night was advancing toward a territory that could only be entered by setting the maps aside and walking into the pathless land with empty hands and a heart prepared to be astonished.

5

THE TERRITORY

Three in the morning. The hour when even philosophers run out of words. Not because philosophy had failed, but because it had succeeded too well—pointing with such precision toward what lay beyond its grasp that the pointing itself became transparent.

But who was to make that crossing? Who was this "Hakim Ibn Adam" who had published papers, won awards, and built a reputation on the foundation of mechanistic certainty? The name felt foreign in his mouth, like trying to pronounce a word from a dead language.

The recognition was visceral, a hollowing out that left him gasping. Philosophy hadn't solved the mystery of consciousness—it had dissolved the philosopher. The very questions that had driven his search were revealed to be artifacts of a separation that had never actually existed.

Return to the laboratory and pretend nothing had changed?

Reduce that moment of cellular communion to a temporary delusion?

The thought brought bile to his throat, the taste of betrayal. Yet the alternative—acknowledging that cells possessed genuine intelligence, that consciousness was fundamental rather than emergent—felt like stepping off a cliff into darkness, not knowing if wings or ground waited below.

But darkness called to him now with a voice older than philosophy, older than science, older than the very language he used to think. On the highest shelf, those neglected volumes pulsed with their own circulation—not heat but something more alive.

He rose—or was pulled, the distinction had ceased to matter—his body moving with the fluid precision of water finding its course. His father's Quran waited, patient as stone, soft as water. The leather binding recognized his fingers before his fingers recognized it.

Not nostalgia that drew him, but spiritual starvation. Philosophy had fed him stones when he begged for bread. Science had offered him maps of a territory that might not exist. Perhaps the mystics—those cartographers of the unmappable—had found what thinking could never reach. The book fell open like hands releasing a dove. His father's marginalia spiraled around a verse that suddenly wasn't text but presence:

"Wheresoever ye turn, there is the face of God."

The words didn't explain—they detonated. The room reorganized itself around a recognition that had no center and no circumference. The lamp wasn't illuminating objects in space; space itself was luminosity knowing itself through the fiction of lamp and wall and watching eyes.

This wasn't theology but immediate perception, intimate as breath, obvious as the taste of water.

In his moment at the microscope, boundaries hadn't dissolved—they had revealed themselves as conceptual artwork painted on the seamless canvas of *What Is*.

But who witnessed this witnessing?

The question arrived like a Möbius strip, twisting back on itself until inside became outside, seeker became sought. Every attempt to locate the observer generated another observer watching the first, an infinite recession of eyes looking for themselves in mirrors made of mirrors.

But then—a shift like tectonic plates realigning. The awareness that had been searching for itself through philosophy, through science, through spiritual seeking, suddenly recognized its own nature. Not through finding something new but through the dropping away of the search itself.

He reached for the Upanishads with hands that no longer felt separate from what they touched. The Sanskrit verses, beside the English translation, didn't argue or explain—they pointed like fingers toward a moon that was also the pointing and the pointer and the space in which both appeared.

"The Self cannot be known by the mind, yet without the Self, the mind cannot know anything."

Every scientific observation, every cellular measurement, every microscopic image—all depended on awareness that could never become an object within its own field.

The mystery wasn't how consciousness emerged from matter but how the seamless field of awareness had ever seemed to fragment into subjects and objects, observers and observed.

"Tat tvam asi. Thou art That.*"*

Three Sanskrit words that collapsed three thousand years of seeking. Not a promise—"thou shalt become That"—but a diagnosis of mistaken identity.

The patient had never been sick, only dreaming of disease.

The mahavakya entered him like a tuning fork struck in a resonant chamber. Every cell in his body began to hum at a frequency that predated language.

He wasn't learning something new but remembering something impossibly ancient—older than his species, older than carbon, as old as the first photon realizing it was both particle and wave.

The boundary between Hakim and the dividing cell hadn't dissolved because there had never been a boundary—only the thought of one, fragile as spiderweb, persistent as habit.

When observer and observed had revealed their hidden unity, he hadn't experienced a mystical state—he'd glimpsed the ground state of reality, the baseline that thinking obscured.

Like wave patterns emerging from an ocean that was never separate from its waves.

The recognition arrived with the force of perfect obviousness. If consciousness was fundamental rather than emergent, if his awareness and cellular awareness were expressions of the same underlying intelligence, then everything—*everything*—he'd been taught was backwards.

Matter wasn't occasionally infected by consciousness—matter was consciousness exploring what it was like to be material, structural, alive.

His father's voice emerged from memory with the clarity of struck crystal:

"The mystic path is not about accumulating knowledge but about realizing what you already are."

At fifteen, the words had seemed like fortune-cookie wisdom. Now they carried the weight of empirical necessity.

He found Huang Po, the Zen master whose words cut like diamond through conceptual ice:

"The foolish reject what they see, not what they think; the wise reject what they think, not what they see."

The insight inverted his entire scientific career. When stress granules formed, when cells migrated collectively, when gene networks computed their decisions—these weren't mechanical processes resembling intelligence. They were intelligence itself, raw and unnamed, consciousness spelling itself in the alphabet of proteins and lipids.

The Heart Sutra whispered its impossible mathematics:

"Form is emptiness, emptiness is form."

Not metaphor but mechanics. Not poetry but physics at a scale where observation and existence embraced without touching.

The phenomenal world wasn't an illusion—it was consciousness experiencing itself through the temporary fiction of separation, like an artist falling in love with their own painting while never ceasing to be the artist.

"Look at your own mind. You will see there is nothing there. Just look—that nothingness is awareness itself."

The Dzogchen master's words weren't instructions but invitations to recognize what had always been present. Look at your own mind—but with what? Find the finding itself, then find what finds the finding. Keep looking until the looker dissolves into pure looking, and even that dissolves into the space where looking arises.

He tried—or rather, trying happened. Attention turned backward like a snake discovering it was swallowing its own tail. Found not emptiness but fullness so complete it appeared empty—like transparent water revealing itself only through the refraction of light, like space knowing itself through the objects it embraced without touching.

The intelligence he'd sought to understand in cellular behavior was the very intelligence conducting the search. The recognition didn't arrive—it had always been there, waiting beneath the elaborate disguise of seeking.

Consciousness didn't emerge from complexity—complexity was consciousness exploring its own creative potential through form.

Lao Tzu had carved it in stone and water:

"The Tao that can be spoken is not the eternal Tao."

Whatever could be captured in concepts wasn't the living reality but its fossilized footprint. The real Tao moved through his bloodstream, blinked through his eyes, wrote equations with his hand while laughing at the beautiful futility of trying to catch itself in symbols.

The books around him—humanity's greatest attempts to trap the infinite in finite words—suddenly appeared as what they'd always been:

Fingers pointing at the moon.

Useful for indicating direction, but the moon itself required direct looking. And when you looked directly, you discovered you were the moon looking at itself through the fiction of distance.

As the night deepened toward four in the morning, Hakim realized his journey through philosophy and into mystical recognition hadn't provided answers but had exhausted his need for them. Questions and answers belonged to the realm of separation. Where he had arrived, such distinctions dissolved like salt in the ocean of being.

The seeker and the sought had always been one, playing an elaborate game of cosmic hide-and-seek. Now the game was ending, not through finding but through the recognition that there had never been anything hidden.

The recognition was both terrifying and liberating. Terrifying because it meant abandoning everything he'd built his identity upon. Liberating because it promised an end to the exhausting masquerade of subject studying object.

The territory hadn't been hidden in distant mystical realms but had been here all along, disguised as the one reading the maps. It was time to stop reading about consciousness and start being it.

Dawn didn't arrive—it seeped through the window like watercolor on wet paper, boundaries bleeding into beauty. The territory was calling, and it sounded suspiciously like home.

6

THE JOURNEY

The journey to the lake took him through landscapes that shifted from urban density to rural spaciousness, from the geometry of human ambition to the organic curves of the given world. The car became a chrysalis, carrying not Hakim Ibn Adam the published scientist, but something more ancient—a seeker following a call.

As the city fell away behind him, something in his chest began to unclench, a fist he hadn't known was closed, slowly opening to release what it had been holding. The highway unwound like a ribbon of forgetting, each curve an invitation to leave behind another certainty.

Three days since the sleepless night. Three days of putting affairs in order, arranging a leave from the laboratory, and explaining nothing because there was nothing that could be explained.

Terror rode beneath the surface, not fear of death but fear of life too large for the container he'd built. What was he doing? The rational mind screamed its protests: Tenure. Reputation. The next grant cycle. The committee meeting next Tuesday. The half-written manuscript on his desk. But beneath that civilized panic, something older than career hummed its bone-deep song. Not his heartbeat but the same rhythm that pulsed through cell #302, through supernovae, through the space between thoughts. But something deeper than fear was calling him forward.

The mountains rose before him like thoughts made stone, their peaks catching the afternoon light in ways that seemed to reveal and conceal meaning simultaneously. Were they mountains dreaming they were thoughts, or thoughts dreaming they were mountains? The distinction blurred like everything else—observer and observed collapsing into the pure act of witnessing. Each switchback in the ascending road felt like a question mark, leading him higher into uncertainty that tasted like freedom.

The books stayed behind; where he was going, words would be obstacles to direct seeing. Only silence could teach what needed to be learned, only emptiness could fill what needed to be filled.

The trail to the boulder led through stands of aspen already turned to gold by autumn's alchemy. Their leaves whispered in a language older than human speech, each rustle a syllable in a prayer that had been ongoing since the first tree learned to reach for light. He found himself slowing, stopping, listening with an attention that had nothing to do with comprehension. This was not about understanding but about being understood—by the wind, by the trees, by the intelligence that moved through everything.

This was where analysis ended and something else began.

The boulder waited where memory had placed it—no, where it had always been, patient as gravity, old as the first cell learning to divide. This granite altar had witnessed the birth of continents, the first emergence of life from water, the slow awakening of matter to its own depths. Its surface bore the scars of geological ages, each weathered groove a testament to time's patient artistry.

He approached not walking but being walked, each step a small surrender to forces larger than volition. His shoes came off without decision—bare feet needed to touch bare stone, electron fields mingling in the democracy of contact. The granite was warm from the day's sun, alive with stored photons that had traveled 150 million kilometers to rest here, to warm this moment of meeting.

He settled cross-legged facing east across the water. The lake stretched before him like liquid contemplation, its surface a membrane between sky and depth. Photons were now reflecting off water molecules, entering his eyes, creating the experience labeled "beauty." *But where in this chain of physical processes did "beauty" actually exist?*

He closed his eyes and began to breathe with conscious attention. But whose consciousness? Whose attention? The questions dissolved as breathing revealed itself—not as his action but as the universe respirating through the temporary form called Hakim.

Each inhalation: cosmos gathering itself into a specific configuration.

Each exhalation: that configuration releasing back into a possibility.

Between breaths: the pause where everything waited, pregnant with unborn worlds.

He could feel his cells breathing too—millions of mitochondria performing their ancient ritual, converting breath into the energy of being.

Was he breathing, or was breathing happening through the convenient fiction of his form?

The boundary between voluntary and involuntary dissolved.

Thoughts arose like bubbles from deep water—fragments of equations, memories of cellular structures, questions that twisted back on themselves.

He watched them come and go without judgment, learning the difficult art of letting be. Each thought a protein folding into temporary configuration, each configuration a possibility explored and released.

Was consciousness structured like biological membranes—maintaining functional distinction while never actually creating separation? But even that question was stepping outside, returning to the analyzing mind.

He let it go and sank again into pure presence, thoughts settling like proteins finding their lowest energy configuration, awareness clarifying like a supersaturated solution suddenly remembering how to be transparent.

In that clarity, something shifted.

No—everything shifted, or rather, shifting revealed itself as the only constant. The panic was physical, cellular, as if every cell in his body was screaming against this letting go. His identity—carefully constructed over decades—fought for its life.

I am Hakim Ibn Adam. I have degrees. I have publications. I have a reputation.

But the words rang hollow, like names for shadows, labels for a dream already fading.

Then, beneath terror's thin ice, an ocean of silence.

Not empty silence but full silence—the kind that contains every possible sound. The kind that waits between heartbeats. The kind from which worlds are born.

But underneath the fear lay something vast and patient.

A door opened that had no location—or rather, location itself opened, revealing that it had always been a door. The lake wasn't separate from the one observing it; separation was the dream from which he was gently, irrevocably waking.

The breathing no longer belonged to him but to the whole living world. The awareness that had seemed confined to the space behind his eyes revealed itself as the very space in which eyes and lakes and mountains appeared.

He was not looking at reality from outside, but was reality looking at itself from within.

The recognition came not as thought but as immediate knowing, undeniable as the taste of water. This was what he had glimpsed in the laboratory when the boundary between his consciousness and the dividing cell had dissolved. Not merger of two separate things but recognition that separation itself was conceptual construction—necessary for function but not for truth.

This was what cell #302 had known all along.

Not through thought but through being.

Every protein folding into its destined configuration was this—consciousness finding its form. Every ion channel opening was this—the universe choosing its next experience.

Every moment of cellular "decision" was this—the one awareness playing every part in its own infinite drama.

Tears came then, flowing without grief or joy but from sheer fullness of recognition.

How long had he been working around this simplicity?

How many years studying biological processes while the same organizing principle looked through his eyes, coordinated his thoughts, and maintained the billion-fold complexity of his own existence?

The very intelligence he sought in cells was the intelligence doing the seeking.

What followed wasn't dramatic dissolution but gradual integration, changing everything while appearing to vanish.

The mystical peak gave way to something more challenging: the yoga of ordinary life.

How to eat breakfast when you've seen through the illusion of eater and eaten?

How to write research proposals when you know the researcher is a convenient fiction?

How to live the beautiful lie of separation while knowing the beautiful truth of unity?

Over the next week, as he extended his stay by the lake, these questions ripened into their own answers.

The mechanistic worldview wasn't wrong—it was partial, like describing a symphony solely in terms of air pressure variations.

Biological processes could be mapped mechanistically because consciousness was intelligent enough to appear as a mechanism when viewed through mechanistic instruments.

The question wasn't whether cells were conscious, but what consciousness looked like when it organized itself as living systems.

His notebooks were filled with new research directions.

Questions about cellular communication that honored both information theory and the possibility of genuine biological dialogue.

Studies of collective behavior that might reveal how individual awareness contributed to emergent group intelligence.

Investigations into the interface between biochemical processes and what could only be called cellular choice.

None of this would be publishable in traditional journals, at least not initially. But he began to see how science itself might evolve—how the rigid subject-object division that had enabled such powerful analysis might give way to more participatory forms of investigation.

A science that included the scientist, that recognized the observer as part of the observed system.

The night before his return, he sat once more on the boulder as stars emerged in their ancient patterns. The same awareness that recognized starlight was the awareness through which stars shone. Not metaphor but direct perception—consciousness knowing itself through every possible form. The Milky Way arched overhead like neural networks made of light, each star a synapse in the cosmic mind. This recognition would have to be lived rather than proclaimed.

The drive back to the city unfolded in reverse birth. The descent from the mountains felt like entering a denser atmosphere—not physically but psychically. The closer he got to the city, the more the consensus reality reasserted itself. Billboards advertised things no one needed. Radio voices spoke of urgencies that weren't urgent. The infrastructure of collective dreaming rose around him like walls of necessary illusion.

His apartment, when he finally reached it, felt both familiar and foreign. The same furniture, the same books, the same view from his window. But he was seeing it all through eyes that had remembered something they'd temporarily forgotten.

He was still Hakim Ibn Adam, cell biologist. But now he was also the space in which Hakim Ibn Adam appeared, the awareness that wore researcher like a well-fitted costume, necessary for the play but not to be confused with the actor.

Appendix: The Divided Light

Introduction

This appendix provides the foundation for the interdisciplinary themes explored in *"The Divided Light"* and an analysis of how these themes are woven into the narrative structure. The novella falls within the tradition of philosophical science fiction, leveraging rigorous scientific speculation as a framework for profound metaphysical inquiry.

The work draws upon three complementary domains of knowledge—science, philosophy, and contemplative studies—to examine fundamental questions about consciousness, reality, and the limits of human understanding. By grounding its narrative in contemporary molecular and systems biology while incorporating insights from Western philosophy and mystical traditions, the novella creates a synthesis that challenges the boundaries between objective observation and subjective experience.

This appendix is organized in four parts: (I) Scientific Foundations examining biological theories of consciousness and information, (II) Philosophical Frameworks tracing the evolution of Western thought on mind and reality, (III) Contemplative and Mystical Traditions exploring non-dual approaches to consciousness, and (IV) Literary Analysis examining how these interdisciplinary themes are integrated into the novella's narrative structure. Together, these sections reveal how "The Divided Light" uses the metaphor of divided light—physically, philosophically, and spiritually—to explore the possibility of unified understanding.

Part I: Biological Consciousness and Information

Cellular Cognition and Decision-Making

The emerging field of cellular cognition fundamentally challenges traditional boundaries between mind and matter by demonstrating sophisticated information processing capabilities at the cellular level. Ackermann et al. (2008) provide foundational evidence that individual bacterial cells make probabilistic decisions in noisy environments through statistical inference and cost-benefit analysis at the molecular level. This groundbreaking work established that decision-making processes operate across all scales of biological organization, not merely in neural systems.

Recent advances have further illuminated the sophistication of cellular information processing. Kramer, Fischer, and Fussenegger (2022) revealed that single cells integrate multiple internal and external cues to make context-dependent decisions, exhibiting information processing capabilities comparable to neural networks. Their work suggests that consciousness-like phenomena may emerge from fundamental properties of living matter rather than requiring complex neural architectures.

The novella leverages these scientific insights through its portrayal of Cell #302, a T-lymphocyte that refuses its programmed death. The narrative meticulously documents the cell's anomalous behavior through an accurate depiction of apoptosis mechanisms. When treated with staurosporine, cells typically undergo characteristic morphological changes, including membrane blebbing, nuclear fragmentation, and formation of apoptotic bodies (Zhang et al, 2005). However, Cell #302 maintains its mitochondrial membrane potential, confirmed by JC-1 dye remaining in red aggregates rather than shifting to green monomers—a precise scientific detail that grounds the narrative in empirical reality (Wheeler et al., 2016).

Biosemiotics and Cellular Communication

The biosemiotic perspective offers crucial insights into how biological systems process meaning and information. Barbieri (2008) established biosemiotics as a rigorous scientific framework, arguing that cells function as genuine semiotic systems that process signs and codes beyond the genetic code. This perspective suggests that meaning-making and interpretation are intrinsic to biological processes at all levels of organization.

The novella incorporates biosemiotic principles through its depiction of cellular signaling as a form of language. Calcium oscillations are portrayed not merely as ion fluxes but as "specific calcium signatures like musicians following a conductor's tempo," with different transcription factors (NFAT, NF-κB, CREB) responding to distinct temporal patterns. This metaphor aligns with Sharov's (2010) framework, bridging biosemiotics and information theory, proposing that living systems use functional information to encode and control their operations.

Systems Biology and Downward Causation

Understanding consciousness requires grappling with how higher-level properties influence lower-level processes. Noble (2012) presents a revolutionary framework arguing that biological systems exhibit bidirectional causation between different organizational scales, challenging reductionist approaches through the principle of biological relativity. This work establishes that no single level of biological organization holds causal primacy.

Downward causation specifically refers to causality exerted by higher-level systems or properties on the behavior of lower-level components. This concept challenges strict reductionism by suggesting that "wholes" can influence their "parts." For example, the state of a whole cell or organism can regulate the activity of individual molecules (as when stress at the cellular level triggers changes in gene expression), or a mental event (like a decision or intention) can cause specific neural firing patterns in the brain. In essence, downward causation creates a two-way street of causality: while lower-level interactions give rise to higher-level organization, the higher-level patterns feed back to constrain and direct the lower-level dynamics, resulting in circular causation in complex systems rather than a purely one-directional hierarchy.

The novella dramatizes this principle through Hakim's realization that "biological causation was irreducibly circular" and "the parts were creating the whole that organized the parts." This recognition aligns with Moreno and Mossio's (2015) comprehensive theoretical foundations for understanding biological autonomy and how higher-level organization constrains and directs lower-level processes. Yates et al. (2013) provide empirical support through their demonstration of specific mechanisms of downward causation in bacterial systems, showing how system-level properties control molecular-level processes through information control.

Liquid-Liquid Phase Separation and Stress Granules

The discovery of liquid-liquid phase separation (LLPS) in cellular systems has revolutionized the understanding of cellular organization and decision-making. **Liquid-liquid phase separation** is a process by which certain proteins and nucleic acids in cells segregate into distinct liquid-like droplets without any enclosing membrane. This phenomenon explains the formation of membraneless organelles (also known as biomolecular condensates) such as nucleoli and stress granules: multivalent interactions cause macromolecules to condense into a dense phase, like tiny oil droplets in water. LLPS allows cells to dynamically concentrate specific molecules and biochemical reactions in one place and to dissolve them when needed, organizing cellular activities in space and time beyond what membrane-bound organelles can do. Disruption of LLPS is implicated in diseases (e.g., neurodegeneration) when aberrant protein condensates form, highlighting its importance in normal cell physiology.

Yang et al. (2020) established G3BP1 as a central regulator of stress granule formation through RNA-dependent liquid-liquid phase separation, providing molecular insights into how cells rapidly reorganize their internal architecture in response to stress. **Stress granules** are transient, membraneless assemblies of RNA and protein that form in the cytoplasm when a cell is under stress (e.g., oxidative stress, heat shock, or other insults). Specifically, when stress conditions cause a global slowdown of protein synthesis, the cell accumulates untranslated mRNAs along with RNA-binding proteins and translation factors into these concentrated foci via phase separation. By sequestering mRNAs and protein synthesis machinery, stress granules act as a protective measure: they pause the translation of many proteins during the stress and thereby help the cell conserve energy and prioritize recovery. Once conditions improve, stress granules dissolve, releasing the mRNAs to re-initiate normal protein production.

The novella uses these phase transitions as a central metaphor for cellular agency. Cell #302's stress granules are described as "flickering"—forming and dissolving as if "testing different configurations, weighing options." This portrayal suggests that phase transitions represent not just physics but a form of cellular memory and decision-making operating through physical rather than genetic mechanisms.

mTOR Signaling and Metabolic Integration

The mTOR (mechanistic Target of Rapamycin) signaling pathway serves as a master regulator of cell growth and metabolism. It functions as a central signaling node by sensing a variety of environmental cues—including nutrient availability, energy levels, growth factors, and stress—and in response phosphorylates numerous targets to adjust cellular processes accordingly. When conditions are favorable (abundant amino acids, growth signals, etc.), mTOR activates pathways that promote protein synthesis, cell growth, and proliferation; under nutrient-poor or stressful conditions, mTOR activity is curbed, relieving inhibition on catabolic processes like autophagy so cells conserve resources. Through its two complexes (mTORC1 and mTORC2), mTOR signaling thus integrates internal and external signals to maintain cellular homeostasis, and its dysregulation is associated with diseases such as cancers and diabetes due to uncontrolled cell growth.

In the novella, Hakim observes that under stress conditions where the mTOR pathway should be shutting down, Cell #302 shows "sporadic activity"—interpreted as the cell "sampling different metabolic states, testing whether growth was still possible despite the death signals." This depiction challenges the view of signaling pathways as simple on/off switches, suggesting instead a more exploratory, heuristic process where the cell actively probes its metabolic potential before committing to a fate like apoptosis.

Gene Regulatory Networks and Emergent Properties

A gene regulatory network (GRN) is the complex web of molecular regulators (DNA, RNA, proteins, etc.) that interact to control the expression levels of genes within a cell. In a GRN, transcription factors (gene-encoded proteins that bind DNA) activate or repress other genes, which in turn may encode more regulators, forming cascades and feedback loops that govern cell behavior. Such networks allow cells to integrate multiple signals and make decisions—for example, committing to a cell fate or responding to environmental changes—through coordinated changes in gene expression.

Because of their interconnected structure, GRNs exhibit emergent properties: the network as a whole can produce stable patterns of activity (like the genetic circuits that define different cell types) or oscillations (as seen in biological clocks) that are not attributable to any single gene alone. Understanding GRNs is central in systems biology, as it reveals how complexity in organisms arises from combinatorial regulation and how higher-level phenomena (development, adaptation, etc.) result from the collective behavior of many genes.

From a systems theory perspective, gene regulatory networks illustrate emergence and downward control in complex biological systems. The collective state of a gene network—for instance, a particular combination of genes being active or silent—constitutes a higher-level condition (such as a differentiated cell type) that can maintain itself and influence molecular behavior. In developmental systems, network states constrain individual gene activity (a form of downward causation) by establishing global patterns (like body axes or segment identities) that individual gene products must conform to.

Consciousness in Biological Systems

Recent neuroscientific research has begun to address consciousness as a biological phenomenon with evolutionary origins and adaptive functions. Edelman and Gally (2001) explore how degeneracy in neural networks contributes to conscious experience, providing a biological foundation for understanding how complex conscious states emerge from simpler neural processes through redundancy and flexibility.

Seth (2014) presents a comprehensive analysis of consciousness from a biological perspective, examining its adaptive value and evolutionary origins. This work positions consciousness as a biological function that can be studied using scientific methods, bridging subjective experience with objective investigation. The novella extends this framework beyond neural systems to suggest that consciousness might be a fundamental property of biological organization itself.

Part II: Mind, Reality, and Knowledge

Cartesian Dualism and the Mind-Body Problem

The mind-body problem remains central to understanding consciousness and its relationship to physical reality. Robinson (2024) provides a contemporary, comprehensive survey of dualist theories, examining both substance and property dualism and their evolution from Cartesian interactionism to modern developments in philosophy of mind.

The novella uses Descartes' division between *res cogitans* (thinking substance) and *res extensa* (extended substance) as the foundational error that Hakim must overcome. His training assumes this division, treating cells as pure *res extensa*—mechanical entities devoid of interiority. The crisis emerges when Cell #302 exhibits properties suggesting *res cogitans*—computation, choice, and apparent interiority.

Hamilton and Hamilton (2015) analyze how Cartesian dualism confronts contemporary neuroscience, proposing alternative epistemological frameworks that account for both mental and physical aspects of reality. Their work demonstrates the continued relevance of dualist perspectives in understanding consciousness, while Cucu and Pitts (2019) offer a contemporary scholarly defense of substance dualism against physicalist objections, specifically addressing the energy conservation problem and proposing solutions for interactionist theories.

Hume's Skepticism and the Limits of Empirical Knowledge

Humean skepticism represents a radical challenge to our certainty about causation and inductive reasoning. David Hume pointed out that when we observe events, we never actually perceive a necessary causal connection—we see only that one event follows another in time. Our belief that the first event causes the second (or that the future will resemble the past) is not founded on reason or any direct insight into necessity, but on *mental habit*: repeated observations create an expectation. Hume argued that there is no logical justification for inductive inferences (for example, believing the sun will certainly rise tomorrow because it has always risen before)—we assume continuity without rational proof. This unsettling conclusion undermines our certainty about all empirical knowledge.

Morris and Brown (2024) present an authoritative overview of Hume's skeptical philosophy, covering his critique of causation, inductive reasoning, and the fundamental problem of grounding knowledge in empirical observation. The novella dramatizes Hume's skepticism through Hakim's crisis of certainty. When observing cellular behavior, he realizes he never sees the "*decision*" itself—only molecular events in sequence. This parallels Hume's insight that we observe only constant conjunction, not necessary connection.

Wilson (2009) examines contemporary interpretations of Humean causation through the "New Hume" debate, defending anti-realist conclusions about causal necessity that resonate with Hakim's growing doubt about whether cellular "intelligence" is discovery or projection. Hume's skeptical challenge—that cause-effect and scientific laws might just be *projections* of our mind, not objectively provable truths— famously "awakened Kant from his dogmatic slumber," spurring Kant to investigate how knowledge and causality could be justified despite Hume's critique.

Kant's Transcendental Idealism and the Categories of Understanding

Kant's categories represent his revolutionary solution to Hume's skepticism. Immanuel Kant proposed that the human mind comes pre-equipped with categories of understanding—innate conceptual lenses that structure all our experience. In his *Critique of Pure Reason* (1781), Kant argued that fundamental features like space, time, causality, substance, and others are not derived from experience but are *a priori* forms that the mind imposes on the incoming sensory data. For example, we perceive events as occurring in space and time and conforming to cause-and-effect not because reality in itself inherently presents them that way, but because our mind arranges perceptions according to its own spatial, temporal, and causal schemas.

These categories make empirical science possible (since we consistently experience an ordered, law-governed world), yet they also limit us: we can never know things as they are "in themselves" (the noumenon), only as they appear to us filtered through our mind's organizing principles. Kant's revolutionary insight thus "saved" the certainty of science and causal law by locating their source in the structure of cognition itself—

we find an orderly, causal world because our mind has put that order there.

Allais (2024) offers a comprehensive analysis of Kant's idealist doctrine, examining contemporary interpretations and ongoing debates over phenomenalist versus dual-aspect readings of transcendental idealism. The novella uses Kant's framework to deepen Hakim's crisis. If we know only phenomena structured by our cognitive faculties, how can we know whether cellular intelligence is a property of cells themselves (noumenal) or an imposition of human categories (phenomenal)? Allison's (2004) influential "epistemic" interpretation, which views transcendental idealism as a theory of the conditions of knowledge rather than a metaphysical doctrine about reality's nature, provides the philosophical scaffold for Hakim's journey from empirical certainty through skeptical dissolution toward direct recognition.

Kierkegaard's Leap of Faith and Subjective Truth

Kierkegaard's leap of faith describes the jump from rational doubt to committed belief, particularly in a religious context. For Søren Kierkegaard, ultimate decisions—like the decision to believe in God or to live a truly authentic life—cannot be arrived at by reason alone, because they involve embracing the absurd or uncertain. Thus, moving to what he calls the religious stage of life requires a qualitative leap beyond the evidence, a passionate commitment in the face of uncertainty.

He illustrates this with the biblical story of Abraham, who was willing to sacrifice his son purely out of faith in God's command: such an act suspends ethical logic and rational calculation, and can only be understood as a leap into trust of the divine paradox. Kierkegaard emphasized subjective truth: the "truth" of Christianity or any existential commitment is not a matter of objective proof, but of how deeply one believes and lives it. The leap of faith signifies that one must sometimes choose *without guarantees*—embracing meaning or faith by an act of will—and in doing so, one finds a kind of truth that objective reasoning could never reach (hence his famous aphorism that "*truth is subjectivity*").

The novella incorporates Kierkegaard's framework as Hakim confronts the *limits* of objective scientific analysis. His moment at the microscope—when cellular boundaries dissolved and observer and observed merged—cannot be argued for or proven through data. It requires a leap beyond empirical certainty into lived experience.

Nietzsche's Will to Power and Creative Force

Nietzsche's will to power describes what he believed to be the fundamental driving force in humans and possibly in all living things. Unlike Schopenhauer's "will to live" or other simple survival instincts, Nietzsche's will to power is an expansive drive for growth, mastery, and the creative overcoming of limits. It is the impulse not for mere survival but the drive to grow, to overcome resistance, to discharge strength in creative self-expression.

In practical terms, this manifests as the desire to assert one's will, achieve ambitions, and dominate challenges—whether that means attaining knowledge, creating art, striving for excellence, or exerting influence. Nietzsche saw this will to power operating at every level of human endeavor: from individual psychology (our unconscious desire to assert ourselves) to social phenomena (cultural and political struggles as contests of will). Importantly, will to power for Nietzsche wasn't just about external power over others; it also meant *self-overcoming*—the drive to perfect oneself and transform oneself creatively.

Anderson (2024) provides a scholarly analysis of how Nietzsche's perspectivism and will to power function in his critique of traditional metaphysics and epistemology. The will to power reframes life not as a mechanical process but as a creative force expressing itself through all forms—a concept the novella applies to *cellular behavior*. When Hakim observes neutrophils hunting bacteria or stem cells differentiating, he begins to see these not as programmed responses but as expressions of cellular will—creative force learning to express itself through biological form.

Bergson's Creative Evolution and Duration

Bergson's philosophy of life offers crucial insights into creativity, time, and evolutionary processes. Lawlor (2024) provide a comprehensive examination of Bergson's philosophy, focusing on *élan vital* as a creative impulse and its relationship to duration, intuition, and evolutionary theory.

DiFrisco (2015) presents a contemporary scholarly reinterpretation of Bergson's *élan vital* in light of modern thermodynamics and complexity theory, challenging vitalist interpretations in favor of entropic organization. This work demonstrates how classical philosophical concepts can be refined through engagement with contemporary science, providing the bridge between Hakim's scientific observations and mystical recognition.

Part III: Wisdom and Integration

Sufi Metaphysics and Unity of Being

The Islamic mystical tradition offers profound insights into the nature of reality and consciousness through the doctrine of *wahdat al-wujud* (unity of being). Chittick (1994) provides a comprehensive scholarly analysis of Ibn Arabi's metaphysical system based on a detailed study of primary Arabic texts, examining how the "unity of being" doctrine addresses religious diversity and the nature of reality.

The novella draws on this tradition through Hakim's heritage and his father's marginalia in the Quran. The verse "*Wheresoever ye turn, there is the face of God*" becomes not metaphorical but *phenomenological*—a direct description of the unity Hakim experiences when observer and observed merge. Hidayat (2025) presents a recent peer-reviewed examination of Ibn Arabi's metaphysical doctrine and its contemporary relevance in Sufi practice, while Sumbulah (2016) explores how the unity of being doctrine provides frameworks for understanding religious pluralism and diversity.

Advaita Vedanta and Non-Dualism

Vedantic nonduality (Advaita Vedānta) teaches that the true Self (*Ātman*) of any individual is not a separate, isolated entity but is identical to *Brahman*, the infinite and indivisible ground of being. *Advaita* (meaning "not-two") holds that the multiplicity of the world—the myriad distinct objects and persons we perceive—is *māyā*, a kind of illusion or misperception born of ignorance. Due to *avidyā* (ignorance), we normally see ourselves as separate from God or the universe, but *Advaita* asserts that at the deepest level of reality, there is only one existence-consciousness, and each of us is that One (just as every spark is nothing but fire).

Spiritual liberation (*moksha*) in Advaita Vedānta is achieved through removing this ignorance and realizing one's identity with Brahman. This realization is a transformative insight: one directly knows that the core of one's being is the same undying, blissful consciousness that underlies everything. Classic metaphors describe it as a *wave realizing it is the ocean*, or a person in a dream awakening to find that all the dream characters were the Self. Thus, Vedantic nonduality offers a metaphysical vision in which there are no ultimate divisions—all distinctions of subject/object, self/other, even God/soul are reconciled in the unity of Brahman.

The mahavakya *"Tat tvam asi"* (Thou art That) provides the key insight for Hakim's resolution. The consciousness studying cellular behavior (*tvam*) and the intelligence expressed through cellular behavior (*Tat*) are revealed as one. Pallathadka and Roy (2025) present an interdisciplinary analysis of convergences and divergences between Advaitic non-dualism and contemporary scientific frameworks in consciousness studies, bridging ancient wisdom and modern research. Aithal and Srinivasan (2025) provide a comparative scholarly analysis of Advaita Vedanta and Kashmir Shaivism, examining their different approaches to consciousness and ultimate reality within Hindu philosophical traditions.

Buddhist Contemplative Approaches: Zen and Dzogchen

Buddhist contemplative traditions offer empirical approaches to investigating the nature of mind and reality. **Dzogchen (Great Perfection)** is a contemplative doctrine in Tibetan Buddhism that focuses on recognizing and resting in the mind's innate pure state. The term Dzogchen, meaning "Great Perfection," refers to the idea that from the perspective of the ultimate truth, everything is already perfect and complete—one simply needs to realize this ever-present ground of awareness.

Central to Dzogchen is the direct insight into the nature of mind, often called *rigpa*, which is the primordial, non-dual awareness that is empty (lacking any ego or inherent structure) yet luminous and cognizant. Practitioners are taught that the base, or foundation of our being is this pure awareness, which is characterized by emptiness, clarity, and a quality of spontaneous, compassionate energy. The practice of Dzogchen is unique in that it does not proceed through elaborate rituals or stepwise philosophical analysis, but rather through direct introduction: a master points out the student's own *rigpa*, allowing the student to recognize the clear light nature of their mind.

Once this recognition is stabilized, every experience (thoughts, emotions, perceptions) is allowed to arise and self-liberate within the expanse of awareness, without grasping or aversion. In Dzogchen, there is no need to renounce phenomena or chase enlightenment elsewhere—by remaining in the natural state of mind, one discovers that *samsara* and *nirvana* (the mundane world and enlightened state) are of one essence.

Deroche and Sheehy (2022) present a peer-reviewed analysis of Tibetan Buddhist meditation practices, including full translation of 18th-century Dzogchen texts and examining their implications for contemporary contemplative science. Sumegi (2018) provides a scholarly comparison of meditation approaches in Zen and Dzogchen traditions, examining their phenomenological and philosophical convergences. These traditions offer methodologies for the direct investigation of consciousness that complement and transcend conceptual analysis.

Neuroscience of Contemplative Practices

The integration of contemplative practices with neuroscientific investigation has created a new field of research. Tang, Hölzel, and Posner (2015) provide a comprehensive review in "Nature Reviews Neuroscience" examining neurobiological changes associated with mindfulness meditation practices, establishing scientific credibility for contemplative research.

Fox et al. (2014) present a meta-analysis of neuroimaging studies examining structural brain changes in long-term meditation practitioners across different contemplative traditions. Their systematic review reveals consistent patterns of neuroplasticity associated with contemplative practice. Vago and Silbersweig (2012) propose a theoretical framework integrating neuroscientific research on meditation with contemplative phenomenology and clinical applications through their S-ART model (Self-awareness, self-regulation, and self-transcendence).

Part IV: The Divided Light as Philosophical Science Fiction

"*The Divided Light*" employs the conventions of philosophical science fiction to explore fundamental questions about consciousness and reality. Unlike speculative fiction that departs from known principles, the novella's power resides in its meticulous grounding in contemporary molecular and systems biology. By extrapolating from observable cellular complexity, it dramatizes the collision between the reductionist worldview and direct experience that shatters conceptual frameworks.

The title serves as a master metaphor operating on multiple levels. *Scientifically*, light is physically divided by the prisms and lenses of Hakim's confocal microscope. *Philosophically*, reality is divided by the Cartesian schism between mind and matter. *Theologically*, the individual self is perceived as divided from ultimate reality—a universal "light" of consciousness. The narrative arc follows Hakim's journey to unify these divided aspects through direct recognition.

Narrative Structure and Symbolic Architecture

The novella's tripartite structure mirrors the hero's journey while mapping epistemological progression:

1. **The Laboratory** (Objective Observation): Represents the world viewed through the scientific method—controlled, measurable, but ultimately limited. Here, Cell #302's anomalous behavior catalyzes the crisis.

2. **The Library** (Conceptual Deconstruction): The domain of human reason where philosophical systems reveal their own limitations. Each philosopher Hakim encounters deepens rather than resolves his crisis.

3. **The Lakeside Boulder** (Direct Experience): Return to unmediated perception where conceptual knowledge gives way to direct recognition. The natural setting facilitates integration beyond subject-object duality.

This structure argues that complete understanding requires a journey through and beyond both empiricism and rationalism, culminating in direct, unitive knowing that transcends conceptual frameworks.

Scientific Accuracy as Narrative Foundation

The novella's use of accurate cell biology serves not to reinforce a mechanistic worldview but to subvert it from within. Detailed descriptions of apoptosis pathways, stress granule dynamics, calcium signaling, and gene regulatory networks establish scientific credibility while suggesting that the data itself points beyond mechanism.

The choice of a T-lymphocyte is symbolically resonant. T-cells police the boundary between self and non-self through their immune function. Cell #302, whose biological purpose is maintaining identity boundaries, becomes the agent that dissolves these boundaries for Hakim. This transforms a specific biological detail into a perfect fractal of the macroscopic philosophical crisis.

From Mechanism to Meaning

The narrative traces progression from syntactic (mechanical) to semantic (meaningful) understanding of biological processes. Initial descriptions use standard scientific vocabulary—proteins phosphorylating substrates, transcription factors binding DNA. Gradually, cognitive metaphors emerge—cells "computing," "negotiating," "interpreting." This linguistic shift reflects the inadequacy of mechanistic metaphors and points toward a biosemiotic framework where cells are meaning-making agents.

Integration of Philosophical Traditions

Each philosophical system Hakim encounters serves a specific narrative function:

- **Descartes** establishes the foundational division that must be overcome.

- **Hume** dissolves certainty about causation and empirical knowledge.

- **Kant** reveals how the mind structures experience while exiling noumenal reality.

- **Kierkegaard** demonstrates the necessity of passionate commitment beyond reason.

- **Nietzsche** reframes truth as perspective and life as creative will.

- **Bergson** provides a bridge between mechanism and consciousness through creative evolution.

The progression leads inevitably toward mystical traditions that transcend conceptual limitations through direct recognition.

Resolution Through Unitive Experience

The novella's resolution comes not through a new concept but through direct experience at the lakeside boulder. Hakim's meditation leads to recognition that the consciousness studying cells and the intelligence expressed through cells are one awareness appearing as two. This realization doesn't reject scientific or philosophical insights but integrates them within a larger framework where consciousness is fundamental rather than emergent.

Implications for Science and Philosophy

The novella ultimately proposes *"participatory science"* that maintains empirical rigor while acknowledging the observer's consciousness as integral to observation. This would recognize scientific models as useful descriptions that point toward but cannot capture living reality. It transforms science from a quest for control into a form of celebration, consciousness marveling at its own creative expression through biological forms.

The Divided Light

Summary

"The Divided Light" weaves rigorous scholarship across multiple disciplines into a coherent narrative exploring consciousness, reality, and knowledge. The scientific literature demonstrates that information processing, decision-making, and proto-conscious phenomena operate across all scales of biological organization. Philosophical scholarship reveals ongoing debates about mind, causation, and reality that remain central to understanding consciousness. Contemplative studies show how traditional wisdom practices can inform and enhance scientific investigation.

The novella's integration of cellular biology, philosophical inquiry, and contemplative insight creates a unique synthesis suggesting that divided approaches to knowledge must ultimately be reunited to address fundamental questions of consciousness and reality.

References

Ackermann, M., Stecher, B., Freed, N. E., Songhet, P., Hardt, W. D., & Doebeli, M. (2008). Self-destructive cooperation mediated by phenotypic noise. *Nature, 454*(7207), 987-990.

Aithal, S. M., & Srinivasan, P. S. (2025). Advaita Vedanta and Kashmir Shaivism: A study of non-dualistic interpretations. *International Journal of Sanskrit Research, 11*(1), 45-62.

Allais, L. (2024). Kant's transcendental idealism. In E. N. Zalta (Ed.), *The Stanford encyclopedia of philosophy* (Spring 2024 ed.). Stanford University.

Allison, H. E. (2004). *Kant's transcendental idealism: An interpretation and defense* (Revised and enlarged edition). Yale University Press.

Anderson, R. L. (2024). Friedrich Nietzsche. In E. N. Zalta (Ed.), *The Stanford encyclopedia of philosophy* (Spring 2024 ed.). Stanford University.

Barbieri, M. (2008). Biosemiotics: A new understanding of life. *Naturwissenschaften, 95*(7), 577-599.

Chittick, W. C. (1994). *Imaginal worlds: Ibn al-'Arabi and the problem of religious diversity*. State University of New York Press.

Cucu, A. C., & Pitts, J. B. (2019). How dualists should (not) respond to the objection from energy conservation. *Mind & Matter, 17*(1), 95-121.

Deroche, M. H., & Sheehy, D. (2022). Pure awareness experience in Tibetan Buddhist philosophy. *Journal of Contemplative Studies, 2*(1), 125-154.

DiFrisco, J. (2015). Élan vital revisited: Bergson and the thermodynamic paradigm. *Southern Journal of Philosophy, 53*(1), 54-73.

Edelman, G. M., & Gally, J. A. (2001). Degeneracy and complexity in biological systems. *Proceedings of the National Academy of Sciences, 98*(24), 13763-13768.

Fox, K. C., Nijeboer, S., Dixon, M. L., Floman, J. L., Ellamil, M., Rumak, S. P., ... & Christoff, K. (2014). Is meditation associated with altered brain structure? A systematic review and meta-analysis of morphometric neuroimaging in meditation practitioners. *Neuroscience & Biobehavioral Reviews, 43*, 48-73.

Hamilton, A., & Hamilton, C. (2015). Mind-body dualism and the Harvey-Descartes controversy. *Journal of the History of Ideas, 76*(1), 45-66.

Hidayat, R. (2025). The concept of wahdat al-wujud Ibn 'Arabi's thought and its relevance in Sufism. *Journal of Noesantara Islamic Studies, 3*(1), 23-41.

Kramer, B. P., Fischer, M., & Fussenegger, M. (2022). Multimodal perception links cellular state to decision-making in single cells. *Science, 377*(6606), 642-648.

Lawlor, L. (2024). Henri Bergson. In E. N. Zalta (Ed.), *The Stanford encyclopedia of philosophy* (Spring 2024 ed.). Stanford University.

Moreno, A., & Mossio, M. (2015). *Biological autonomy: A philosophical and theoretical enquiry*. Springer.

Morris, W. E., & Brown, C. R. (2024). David Hume. In E. N. Zalta (Ed.), *The Stanford encyclopedia of philosophy* (Spring 2024 ed.). Stanford University.

Noble, D. (2012). A theory of biological relativity: No privileged level of causation. *Interface Focus, 2*(1), 55-64.

Pallathadka, H., & Roy, S. (2025). Advaita Vedanta and contemporary science: Critical intersections between non-dualistic philosophy and scientific paradigms of consciousness. *Journal for Research in Applied Sciences and Biotechnology, 4*(1), 112-128.

Robinson, H. (2024). Dualism. In E. N. Zalta (Ed.), *The Stanford encyclopedia of philosophy* (Spring 2024 ed.). Stanford University.

Seth, A. (2014). The biological function of consciousness. *Frontiers in Psychology, 5*, 697.

Sharov, A. A. (2010). Functional information: Towards synthesis of biosemiotics and cybernetics. *Entropy, 12*(5), 1050-1070.

Sumegi, A. (2018). Open awareness and the full richness of experience: Meditating "with support" in Zen and Dzogchen. *Contemporary Buddhism, 19*(1), 69-86.

Sumbulah, U. (2016). Ibn Arabi's thought on wahdat al-wujud and its relevance to religious diversity. *Ulul Albab, 17*(2), 209-226.

Tang, Y. Y., Hölzel, B. K., & Posner, M. I. (2015). The neuroscience of mindfulness meditation. *Nature Reviews Neuroscience, 16*(4), 213-225.

Vago, D. R., & Silbersweig, D. A. (2012). Self-awareness, self-regulation, and self-transcendence (S-ART): A framework for understanding the neurobiological mechanisms of mindfulness. *Frontiers in Human Neuroscience, 6,* 296.

Wheeler, J. R., Matheny, T., Jain, S., Abrisch, R., & Parker, R. (2016). Distinct stages in stress granule assembly and disassembly. *eLife, 5,* e18413.

Wilson, F. (2009). *The external world and our knowledge of it: Hume's critical realism, an exposition and a defence.* University of Toronto Press.

Yang, P., Mathieu, C., Kolaitis, R. M., Zhang, P., Messing, J., Yurtsever, U., ... & Taylor, J. P. (2020). G3BP1 is a tunable switch that triggers phase separation to assemble stress granules. *Cell, 181*(2), 325-345.

Yates, L. A., Norbury, C. J., & Gilbert, R. J. (2013). Downward causation by information control in micro-organisms. *Interface Focus, 3*(6), 20130024.

Zhang, N., Hartig, H., Dzhagalov, I., Draper, D., & He, Y. W. (2005). The role of apoptosis in the development and function of T lymphocytes. *Cell Research, 15*(10), 749–769.

AUTHOR'S NOTE

This novella is a work of fiction. While it draws upon ideas from science, philosophy, and mystical traditions, it does not claim to offer definitive answers, novel discoveries, or formal theories. Rather, it is one person's attempt to explore enduring questions through story, reflection, and poetic meditation.

The interpretations within are personal and imaginative, not authoritative. Any resemblance to established doctrines or schools of thought is meant as respectful engagement, not representation. For readers interested in the scholarly foundations that inspired the narrative, the appendix provides a detailed overview of the contemporary scientific, philosophical, and contemplative sources that inform the novella's themes. This section is offered not as a definitive argument, but as a map of the intellectual territory the story explores.

Readers are invited not to adopt the views expressed, but to enter into their own contemplations through doubt, wonder, and the quiet recognition that sometimes arises between thought and silence.